Oliver
and his
Magical Cloud Paradise

story by

ANNEKARIEN VAN DE VELDE
ILLUSTRATIONS BY JEANNE EE WEI YEN

Balboa Press books may be ordered through booksellers or by contacting:

Balboa Press
A Division of Hay House
1663 Liberty Drive
Bloomington, IN 47403
www.balboapress.com.au
1 (877) 407-4847

ISBN: 978-1-5043-1492-3 (sc)
ISBN: 978-1-5043-1493-0 (e)

Print information available on the last page.

Balboa Press rev. date: 10/25/2018

BALBOA.
PRESS
A DIVISION OF HAY HOUSE

To my dear boy in the clouds

This is Oliver. If you saw him, you would not find anything unusual about him. Oliver is a cheerful boy with twinkling eyes. He likes to laugh. And when he does, he throws his head back and squeezes his eyes shut and then he laughs heartily. It is such a contagious laugh. A laugh that makes everyone laugh, even if only a little bit.

Oliver may seem like an ordinary boy, but he does not live like other people. Oliver lives in the clouds. Oliver calls it 'Cloud Paradise'. He lives there together with his mother and father. It has always been like this. Or at least for as long as Oliver can remember. Their house is in the middle of the clouds and has a beautiful view of the Earth.

Clouds change from grey clouds to fluffy clouds, from cumulus clouds to rain clouds, and sometimes there is not a cloud to be seen. Have you ever noticed this? But please do not worry: Oliver's house is always sitting on a cloud. It does not go away. Oliver loves this about his house.

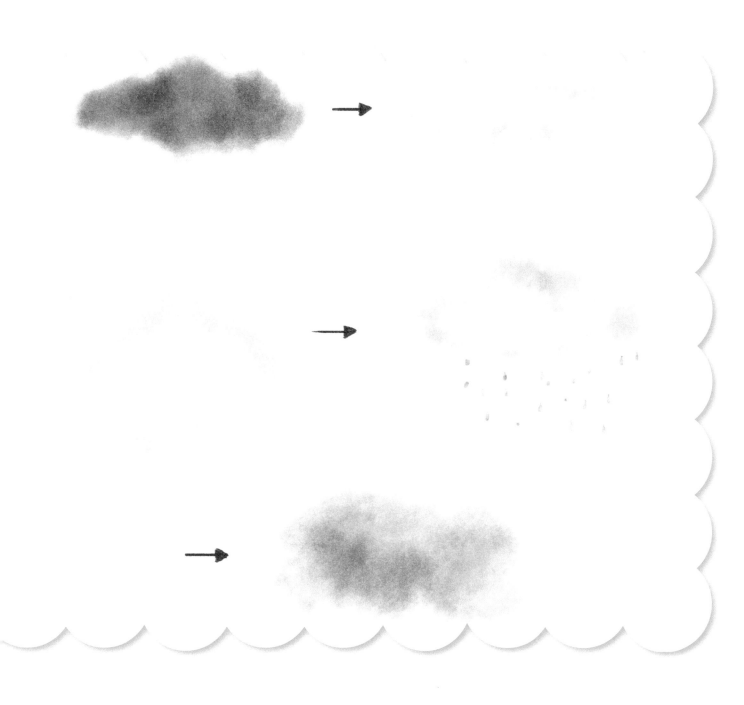

It is the first day of the week: Monday. It is morning and the sun is awake like Oliver. Her rays of light shine brightly. Oliver lies on a white fluffy cloud. The cloud feels warm and soft and it tickles his feet a bit.

Oliver carefully shuffles forward to the edge of the cloud and looks down to the Earth. There he sees cars driving, people cycling and children playing on the beach. Oliver especially loves looking at beaches, because the people seem to be so relaxed there!

Oliver is always a bit curious about life on Earth. What would it be like to live over there? But please do not think that Oliver is lonely in Cloud Paradise! Many children live there and Oliver has lots of friends.

Oliver and his friends often play together on the clouds. They play tag, hide and seek, they bike and much more! Oliver plays the most with Suki, because Suki is his best friend.

The people on Earth like it when the sun shines. But Oliver and Suki love a sky that is cloudy. Then there are many clouds on which to play.

Today it is the second day of the week: Tuesday. It is cloudy. 'Great!' says Oliver excitedly. He is going to pick up Suki . 'Shall we play tag?' asks Oliver. 'Yes!' Suki answers.

Oliver and Suki love to play tag. This is one of their favourite games. 'Tag, you are it!' shouts Oliver and he quickly jumps from one cloud to another. Suki jumps after him, but she stumbles and ends up with her face in a cloud. Her face is completely white from the cloud! Oliver and Suki have to laugh at Suki's white cloud-face.

It is the third day of the week: Wednesday. Wednesday is always a fun day in Cloud Paradise. On this day there are a lot of aeroplanes passing by. When an aeroplane passes, the children can bike on the white trails left by the aeroplane. Oliver, Suki and their friends wait with their bikes for an aeroplane to arrive.

And yes, there is one! It is a big one, which leaves a beautiful thick white trail. Perfect for an aeroplane race! 'Who can chase the aeroplane the fastest? Ready, steady, go!' Oliver shouts. The children all jump on their bikes and start the chase. It is an exciting race. Oliver and Suki go equally fast but in the end Suki wins. 'Well done Suki!' says Oliver and he gives Suki a high five.

It has been raining in Cloud Paradise. For a while rain can be fun, but it is not Oliver's favourite thing. It is the fourth day of the week: **Thursday**. The rain has stopped. Oliver wakes up and sees cumulus clouds from his bedroom window.

'Fantastic, cumulus clouds!' says Oliver when he enters the living room. Mother laughs at Oliver's excited greeting. 'Good morning to you, too' she says while she gives Oliver a hug. 'Have your breakfast and then you can go and play outside.'

When there are cumulus clouds Oliver and Suki often go sledging. They climb all the way up to the highest cloud and then they go *zoof zoof* with their sledges to the bottom of the cloud.

Oliver and Suki head up the cumulus clouds. 'Shall we go together on the sledge?' asks Suki. 'Great idea!' Oliver replies. They climb together onto the big timber sledge that Suki's father built last year. 'Ready, steady, go!' Oliver calls and the two sledge down.

Oh dear, how fast they go! Oliver almost falls off the clouds. The bottom cloud has to catch Oliver. Fortunately, the clouds pay good attention and will always catch the children with their strong cloud hands. 'Thank you cloud!' Oliver says. And Oliver and Suki climb the cumulus clouds to have another go. Oh... how wonderful cumulus clouds are!

It is the fifth day of the week: **Friday**. There are many fluffy clouds. Oliver and Suki love fluffy clouds. They are just as much fun as snow because they can build figures from the clouds. They are like snowmen, but made of clouds: cloudmen!

All the children join in and they make very big cloudmen. They build a cloudman in the shape of a butterfly, one in the shape of a giant teddy bear with a tuxedo, another in the shape of a fluffy bunny with thick woollen fur and Oliver and Suki build a super fast cloud pirate ship.

The children are finished and admire their cloudmen. 'Look!' Suki shouts. She points down to a boy and a girl on Earth. They are standing in a small garden and they look up at the skies. The boy is pointing at the cloudmen. Oliver and Suki are very proud of themselves.

Do you ever look at the clouds? Pay attention, because next time you are sure to spot cloudmen!

It is the sixth day of the week: Saturday. It is raining in Cloud Paradise. The skies are grey and there are no clouds to play on. Oliver and Suki are at home. Mother has made them a lovely cup of tea. And now Oliver and Suki wait for the rain to stop and the white fluffy clouds to appear again.

It is the seventh and last day of the week: Sunday. The sun appears and shines brightly through the rain. A beautiful rainbow appears, because sunlight combined with rain creates a rainbow. And rainbows are Oliver's favourite! There is just nothing like a rainbow.

Oliver and Suki run outside towards the rainbow. All the children follow in their tracks. They pick a coloured line. Oliver chooses red and Suki chooses orange. And they all go *zoof zoof* down the rainbow slide! Oliver, Suki and their friends slide ten times from the rainbow and then they lie down in the fluffy clouds. What a wonderful day!

Do you see a rainbow sometimes? When you do, pay attention.
You might see Oliver and Suki slide down! And when you see them,
please be sure to wave to them. They are certainly waving back.

About the author

Annekarien loves writing calming stories for children and expanding their imagination. Annekarien was born in the Netherlands and currently resides in New Zealand with her husband and their three children.

About the illustrator

Jeanne Ee is an illustrator and graphic designer who spends most of her free time illustrating. Amongst all types of illustrations that she does, she loves illustrating children's books best. Jeanne lives in Kuala Lumpur, Malaysia.

Printed in the United States
By Bookmasters